# Three Paws

KAREN STRUCK

PAGE PUBLISHING, INC.
New York, NY

First originally published by Page Publishing, Inc. 2019

ISBN 978-1-64462-752-5 (Paperback)
ISBN 978-1-64462-790-7 (Hardcover)
ISBN 978-1-64462-753-2 (Digital)

Printed in the United States of America

"To my husband, Steve, who is a continuous source of happiness and positivity. I love you!"

Once upon a time, in the land of snowcapped peaks and emerald-green waterfalls, there lived an Alaskan brown bear named Boots. The grizzly bear cub was named for his muddy paws.

"Boots," Mother Grizzly fussed, "how many times have I asked you to stay away from the riverbank?" She glanced at his left front paw, dangling lifeless above the ground. "I thought you learned your lesson that rivers and waterfalls are dangerous!"

Boots lowered his head. "I know, Mother," he grumbled. "How can I catch salmon if I don't go in the water?" He closed his eyes and recalled the day of his accident. Boots and his sister, Chinook, strolled along the riverbank, between magnificent mountain peaks.

\* \* \*

"I dare you to walk to the center of the river with me," Boots yelled as he slowly approached the rapidly moving water. *If I could swim through rapids*, thought Boots, *I could catch salmon as they swim upstream to lay their eggs!* Salmon season was three weeks away, and his greatest dream was to become the best salmon catcher in Ketchikan, Alaska.

"You're nuts!" Chinook shouted as she stood on her back legs and glared at Boots.

"Don't you remember… Mother made us promise not to go into the river without her?"

Boots neared the center of the river. His heart pounded as he tiptoed over moss-covered rocks beneath the rapidly moving water. Without warning, he slipped and splashed onto his back.

"Help!" Boots screamed as he plunged over a twenty-foot waterfall, into the foaming waters below. He gasped for air.

Minutes later, Boots floated to the edge of the riverbank. He was unable to move his left front paw, for his bones had been crushed like a bag of pretzels.

* * *

"It's been two months since your accident!" Mother Grizzly said. "How are you going to survive on your own with only three paws? As long as you're living with me, you will not *go* into the river!"

"That's not fair!" Boots said. "The other cubs will think I'm a baby."

"You broke your promise to me," she sighed, "and look what happened!"

Boots left the den. As he walked past sedges and horsetails along the river, Boots heard a thunderous rumble from the mountaintop. He looked up the steep slope and saw a goat tumbling down the jagged cliff. The goat landed with a thud. His back leg injured as he cried out in pain. Boots sprinted toward the goat, looming over him.

"Oh please, don't eat me!" the goat begged tearfully. Boots was reminded of his own accident.

"Why shouldn't I eat you?" Boots asked. He knew if he didn't take the goat home as dinner, another bear, wolf, or coyote would come along and eat the goat.

"I'll make you a promise," the goat offered. "If you'll help me climb back up the mountain, I promise you a salmon feast one week from today!"

"That's impossible!" Boots said.

"It's true!" The goat reassured him. "I have friends in high places, and they owe me a favor."

The goat eyed Boots' dangling paw. He knew catching salmon could be difficult for the bear cub.

"How would you like to become the greatest salmon catcher in all of Ketchikan? I've been watching bears catch salmon for years," the goat said. "I know their tricks!"

Boots' eyes twinkled. "If you can teach me how to catch salmon… I'll help you!"

20

Boots supported the goat's back legs using his head, like a chair, as they crawled back up the mountain.

When Boots returned to the riverbank, a snarling grizzly bear cub glared at him.

"Wait until I tell the other bears what you've done!" Grizzwald shouted. "That goat should be our dinner tonight!" He growled at Boots, exposing his sharp teeth and white claws, the length of a human finger.

"The goat promised us a salmon feast one week from today if I helped him up the mountain," Boots explained as he slowly backed away from the angry cub.

"And you believed that old goat?" he hissed. Grizzwald spun around and stomped off.

* * *

Over the next week, the goat taught Boots how to charge upstream and downstream, frightening the fish and swatting them onto the gravel bars. He learned how to swim underwater and snatch the fish between his jaws. Boots felt alive again!

By week's end, all the bears gathered along the river. Grizzwald's father, a thousand-pound grizzly, towered above Boots.

"Where's your *goat* friend?" he growled angrily. "If he doesn't keep his promise, I'll be eating *you* for dinner!"

Boots felt like a million butterflies fluttered in his stomach. He wondered how a mountain goat could keep such a promise. He remembered the goat saying, "I have friends in high places."

Suddenly, one of the bears shouted, "Look up, everyone!"

Dozens of bald eagles soared above them, clutching fresh salmon between their sharp talons. Hundreds of salmon dropped to the ground. Bears scattered in all directions, gripping salmon between their strong jaws.

Mother Grizzly raced to her cub, nuzzling against his fur. "This is a miracle," she gushed. "How did you make this feast possible?"

31

Boots looked up to the mountaintop and smiled at the goat. "I happen to have friends in high places," he said.

A salmon landed at his feet, flipping and flopping on the ground.

Mother Grizzly knew Boots had been spending more time by the river. "You know how much I worry about you near waterfalls," she sighed disapprovingly.

"That's like asking salmon not to swim upstream," Boots said. "Deep down, they know they have to. It's what salmon do naturally. Catching salmon is what bears do naturally."

Mother Grizzly smiled. She knew he was right.

Boots stood upright, balancing on his back paws. "One day," he said, beaming with pride, "I will be the best three-pawed salmon catcher in all of Ketchikan!"

The End.

# About the Author

**K**aren Struck discovered the joy of children's literature as she read to her daughter each night. She was inspired by the Harry Potter book series and decided to take writing courses at the Institute of Children's Literature. During an Alaskan cruise, the naturalist on board described the dangers faced by billy goats who live along the mountain peaks. They sometimes lose their footing on loose gravel and roll down the mountain cliff, injured and unable to return to the mountaintop. They become prey/dinner for the bears, wolves, and coyotes that linger along the riverbank. As one of her writing assignments, Karen decided to turn an otherwise sad wildlife story into a story of hope, perseverance, and friendship.

Karen is a registered nurse and works in the aesthetic industry, performing laser treatments combined with injectables for skin rejuvenation. She works with her husband, Steve, a plastic surgeon in Atherton, California. She has a daughter named Rachel and two stepchildren, Danni and Evan Struck.